Feb 5, 2000

To Travis

We wish you a wonderful life on the beaches of Chatham and look forward to following your adventures. You are part of a very special family and we love you all.

Lots of love,

Paula + John

Billy's Bird-day

A Young Boy's Adventures on the Beaches of Cape Cod

by

Peter Trull

Peter Trull

ILLUSTRATED BY PAUL ROWNTREE

SHANK PAINTER PUBLISHING • PROVINCETOWN • CAPE COD

For Carol

Book design by Gillian Drake

Published by
SHANK PAINTER PUBLISHING COMPANY
Box 2001, Provincetown, MA 02657
(508) 487-9169

Library of Congress Cataloging-in-Publication Data
Trull, Peter.
    Billy's Bird-day : a young boy's adventures on the beaches of
Cape Cod/by Peter Trull ; illustrated by Paul Rowntree.
    p. cm.
    Includes biographical references.
    SUMMARY: Billy learns about the fragile balance of nature from
two bird wardens, who help him to understand the behavior of Cape
Cod terns.

    1. Terns—Juvenile fiction. 2. Cape Cod (Mass.)—Juvenile
fiction. I. Title

PZ7.T7855Bi 1977   [Fic]
                            QB196-40499

ISBN 1-888959-26-6

10 9 8 7 6 5 4 3 2 1

PRINTED IN USA

*A portion of the proceeds
from this book will be
donated to the
Massachusetts Audubon
Society's Coastal
Waterbird Program for the
Protection of Nesting
Terns, Piping Plovers and
Their Habitats.*

From the Author

Boys and Girls, if you like something a lot, do it a lot. If you like to study Nature, spend a lot of time outdoors, looking, asking questions, and then reading about it. If you like sports, play a lot, get good at it! If you are a dancer, dance as much and as well as you can! Working on computers? Keep it up, work at it! Don't let people stop you from doing what you love to do. Be proud of yourself! Show people what you have accomplished.

When I was a boy I loved birds! I still do! People used to say "What's the big deal about birds?" and "Where do you ever expect to get in your life studying birds?" — Well, it's taken me to some of the most beautiful places in the world, from Canada to South America, studying birds, teaching people about birds and writing stories about birds! It's my profession. No matter what anyone said when I was a boy, my parents were always proud that I loved birds. They always stuck by my interest, no matter how strange it seemed to some people. So Moms and Dads, stick by your kids, be proud of the things they love to do. And kids, remember to say "It's my life!"

— PETER TRULL

Billy's Bird-day

"The beach!" said Billy out loud, as he opened his eyes. He was excited!
His family was going to the beach today! He had awoken early on this sunny,
summer morning, and as he lay snug in his bed, listening to a robin singing outside
his window, he wanted to leave right then for the huge, saltwater Atlantic Ocean
beach. He thought about the big waves and the beautiful shells he would find
along the shore, and he imagined the awesome sandcastle he would build, with
seaweed and bird feather flags on top, and a watery moat all around.

Later that morning, after a long drive in the car, Billy and his family arrived at the beach. The parking lot was so full of cars it was hard to find a parking space.

"Everyone in the world must be at the beach today," Billy said to his Dad, as they looked and looked for a place to park the car.

"Don't worry, my boy," said his Dad calmly. "We'll walk to a spot away from all the people, where no one will bother us. We'll have it all to ourselves."

As Billy, his mom and dad, and his thirteen year old sister Sarah walked along the beach, everything they were carrying—the bags of towels, the cooler of food, the beach umbrella, the blanket, the air mattress, and the bag of tools to make sandcastles—all got heavier and heavier.

"Let's just go back to the other crowded place," grumbled Billy's sister Sarah. "I like being around people, and this air mattress is too heavy to carry. Besides, I have to change the tape in my Walkman."

"You're carrying the lightest thing of all," snapped Billy, tired, taking deep breaths after a long walk in the soft sand.

"Well, maybe if YOU didn't have so many TOYS . . ."

"That's enough!" Dad interrupted. "You kids sound like blue jays at the bird feeder. Relax and look at how beautiful it is here."

By now, everyone was pooped! As Billy looked behind him, he saw how far they'd come, with all the people and their beach umbrellas looking like tiny specks in the distance.

"Here's our spot," said Dad finally, as he sat down on the sand. He reached into the cooler, pulled out a soda, and poosch!—opened it up and started drinking.

"Yes, this seems like a good place," said Mom. "Look how beautiful it is here, nothing around but the sand and the sea."

Billy looked around. His Mom was right — nothing but the sand and the sea . . . and ALL THOSE SIGNS! No one ever seems to notice signs. There are signs at school, signs in stores, signs along the road, signs everywhere! And now even at a deserted part of the ocean beach, SIGNS!

TERNS NESTING

DO NOT ENTER

While Mom and Dad spread out the beach blanket and his sister sat down to fix her ponytail, Billy decided to go up to the dunes to read one of the signs that were stuck in the sand. It read: TERNS NESTING — DO NOT DISTURB THESE ENDANGERED BI . . . but before he finished, birds filled the sky around him and his family. Hundreds of birds shrieking "Keeer, keeer, kik, kik, kik, kik, keeer, keeer" dove towards him!

"Whooaah!" screamed Billy. "Run! They're attacking me!"

It was so noisy, his mom and dad quickly moved the blanket and beach stuff farther from the signs. When they did, something amazing happened! As soon as Billy's family moved away and settled down again, all the birds, called terns, also settled down. In fact, after the birds landed back on the sand, they seemed to disappear.

"Cool." Billy changed his position on his towel so that he now sat with his back to the ocean, watching the huge area of sand, beach grass and dunes for signs of the birds. The harder he looked, the more birds he saw. Their feathers blended perfectly with the sand.

"Camouflage," he thought to himself. No wonder there were signs all around these birds — if there were no signs to protect them, people could walk or drive beach buggies right over them, and not even know it!

For a long time, Billy watched the birds. At first, he saw lots of them sitting on the sand, feathers fluffed out, their feet hidden. But as he watched, he saw tiny heads poke out from under the wings of these resting terns, looking at the world around them. Billy sat perfectly still and quiet. Then he saw more birds flying in from the direction of the sea, carrying small fish towards the sandy nesting area.

"They're feeding babies," he whispered to himself as the flat sandy area seemed to come alive with fluffy little squeaking chicks, running open-mouthed towards the fish-carrying adult birds.

"What a busy place," thought Billy, as he watched the chicks gobble down the fish. The adult birds flew off, back towards the ocean, and the chicks became

still again, blending with the sand. Almost invisible!

As Billy watched all the activity, he saw a green pickup truck driving slowly along the beach. The truck stopped and two people got out and picked something up. Billy figured these people must be Park Rangers. They were dressed in uniforms and seemed to be watching the nesting birds very closely. He wasn't sure what the man had picked up, but he was curious. He walked over to the truck.

"Hi!" he said, with a friendly smile.

"Hi, young fella," said the man in the ranger uniform with a hat like Smoky the Bear wears. He had a badge on his arm that said "National Park Service." The lady wore a brown uniform with a floppy hat. The badge on her arm showed a picture of these birds and said "Massachusetts Audubon Society."

"Are you guys Park Rangers?" Billy asked, squinting in the sun as he looked up at them.

"Actually, we're Wardens," said the man. "We work for different organizations, but we have the same duties, to protect the nesting terns and watch over their nesting areas."

"We write in journals and notebooks," continued the woman, "all about the terns' nesting season, which lasts from May until August. The information we

record is called data, and it helps us understand how these birds live."

"But why?" Billy asked, still squinting.

"What's your name kiddo?" the lady asked.

"Billy."

"Well, I'm Marsha, and this is Vern. We're pleased to meet you, Billy. Part of our job is to tell people at the beach about the nesting colonies, and to protect

the birds from being bothered by people, cars, and even pets that come to the beach." Marsha spoke very softly, as if the birds could hear her and wouldn't be scared. "Look here Billy." She showed Billy what Vern had picked up. It was a baby tern that had been killed, squashed by a truck tire. She told Billy that sometimes the baby terns run outside the signs and people driving along the beach don't see them because they blend so perfectly with the sand.

"It's sad, but a lot get killed," said Vern.

"Then why do they let cars and trucks drive here?" asked Billy, as he looked at the tiny limp body, about as big as a tennis ball.

"Well," Vern explained, "The terns have been nesting on these beaches for many years, since the days before beach buggies and families visited the beach for fun, like they do today. These terns nest on sandy beaches and never had to worry about their eggs and babies being driven over or stepped on. But today, people have a right to come here too, and some people don't even know the birds nest here. That's why we're here today, to make people aware of the nesting colony. People like you Billy, and your family over there." He pointed to Billy's mom, dad, and sister who were enjoying the beach and waves.

"And it's not just people that bother the birds, Billy," Marsha continued. "There are also predators, animals that come to the nesting colony to eat the terns, or to feed their own babies. Birds like Great Horned Owls, Marsh Hawks, and gulls, or mammals like red foxes, striped skunks, and raccoons. Even coyotes come to the nesting colony to eat the terns or their eggs."

While the wardens were telling Billy about the terns, they kept looking through their binoculars at the activity in the colony, as if expecting to see one of the predators they were telling him about! Billy got a chance to look through the binoculars at the birds and it was as if a whole new world had opened up to him.

"These are excellent! The birds are so close!" said Billy in a loud whisper.

At least, they seemed to be. He could see the bright orange and black bill of the common terns, and the sharp, yellow bill and little white patch on the forehead of the least terns. How neatly the feathers overlapped on their wings, and how bright were the dark shiny eyes against the black caps on their heads. "Wow!" whispered Billy, to no one in particular. It was much nicer to see the fuzzy little chicks alive in the grass, or near their parents on the sand, where they were safe.

Soon Vern and Marsha had to get going. They gave Billy a small book which told all about the terns and other plants and animals that live on the beach. He thanked them and said maybe he'd see them again next year. He waved a quiet

wave as they drove off, so he wouldn't scare the terns.

Now Billy was alone again watching the nesting birds. His family was nearby, but still far enough away so he could imagine he was the only person for miles around. Billy thought about all the things the Wardens had told him and showed him. He imagined he was a Warden and his job was to watch over these birds and protect them from people and predators. Little did he know that his imaginings would soon turn to reality, for there were other people near the nesting colony that day.

Because the nesting colony was large, about as big as a football field, Billy was unaware of the ruckus that had started way down the beach, near the far end of the nesting area. But as the cries of the birds grew louder and panic spread throughout the colony, Billy saw hundreds, maybe thousands, of terns rise up in a screaming flock. He searched quickly for predators, maybe a skunk or fox, hawk or owl, that may be killing and eating the birds or their eggs.

Instead, he saw three people, a girl, a boy, and a little toddler, walking right through the nesting area. They had ignored the signs and were being mobbed, attacked, maybe even pecked at, by the angry adult terns, which Billy knew were just trying to protect their eggs and baby chicks. He could tell that the children

were scared and confused. He started running down the beach towards the uproar, his heart pounding. The soft sand made running difficult and as he ran he yelled as loud as he could, "Go back! Turn around! Go back!" But his voice was drowned out by the ear-piercing screams of a thousand angry birds.

The boy, who looked about his age, started throwing rocks at the diving birds. Billy felt desperate, he must get the kids' attention! He entered the nesting area to make a shortcut to the three children who were now surrounded by a shrieking flock of white and gray birds. He could see the birds darting this way and that in the air, trying to avoid the stones which, by now, were being thrown by both older kids at their attackers.

He could hear the littlest child crying, louder and louder! Suddenly, Billy realized that on the ground all around him were eggs and chicks, and that he must watch every step he took as he ran towards the three children. Now the adult terns started attacking Billy! To them he was another unwelcome predator, unaware that he was trying to protect them.

"Stop throwing rocks! Put the rocks down!" screamed Billy as he got nearer, his throat burning from yelling, yet still he was not heard through the shrill roar of a thousand angry birds all around them. "Back, go back that way!" he yelled as he

guided the frightened youngsters back the way they had come. "Watch where you step! Eggs! Keep going, past the signs!" Billy seemed to act on instinct, not thinking about what he said, just saying it, as if everything the Wardens Vern and Marsha had taught him earlier that day had become part of him. He had acted wisely and quickly. They would be proud of him. Oh, how he wished they were there right now!

Just as Billy knew they would, the birds settled down, back to their nests,

within a few minutes after they were away from the nesting area. He explained to the older girl and her two brothers who, like Billy, had never seen a tern nesting colony before, all about the nesting birds. He found himself telling them many of the things Vern and Marsha had told him just a short while before. He realized as he spoke how important it is to teach other people about the ways of nature, and how people should try to understand

the way other creatures live, and what they need to survive.

"We're sorry, we didn't know, we would never hurt the birds on purpose," the big sister told Billy.

"I missed them with my rocks," said her brother, looking very guilty.

"Sorry," squeaked the littlest, who looked about four, and was now nestled safely in the arms of his big sister.

Everyone seemed OK, and the children continued on their way, this time walking around the nesting area, away from the signs.

Billy felt proud. He spent the rest of the after-noon playing in the ocean waves. As he did, he real-ized that a whole new world had opened up to him. Watching the terns flying all around him, he saw they were like a lifeline

that connected the land and sea. Back and forth they went, raising a family on the land, but depending on small fish from the ocean to keep that family alive.

He may not have known what terns were before that day, but as he stood watching, knee-deep in cold ocean water, Billy felt like he knew every bird, and that he cared about each one of them. He couldn't wait to get back home, to learn about the birds in his own neighborhood. Maybe his mom and dad would buy him binoculars—for his bird-day!

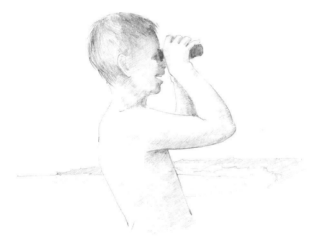

Common Tern
(Sterna hirundo)

The common tern is a gray and white seabird with a black cap, long pointed wings with black tips and a long white forked tail with black along the outer edges. Its beak is bright orange with a black tip. The common terns' legs are bright orange.

Common terns nest in large colonies. They may nest in the beach grass or out on the open beach. Their nest is a shallow scrape in the sand, sometimes made with dead grass which the birds reach out and tuck around them while they incubate the 3 eggs in their clutch. Chicks hatch out in about 23 days. They are fed live fish and shrimp and are able to fly after about 20 days. By August or September, Common Terns get ready to fly south for the winter. They migrate to South America and return to New England again in May. The same pair may nest together for several years.

Least Tern
(Sterna albifrons)

The least tern gets its name from being the least in size. It is a small tern that nests out on the open beaches, sometimes so close to the ocean waves that whole colonies of nests and eggs get washed over in storms. The least tern is grey above and white below and also has a black cap, but this tern has a white patch on its forehead. The least tern has a bright yellow beak with black on the very tip, and yellow legs.

Adults make a shallow scrape in the sand for a nest, and usually lay 2 eggs, which hatch after about 21 days. Like other terns, both parents incubate eggs and care for their young. The chicks are fed small fish which the parents catch by hovering and diving. When they are old enough to fly, they are taught how to fish by their parents. Least terns migrate south in the fall and return to nest in spring.

Arctic Tern

(Sterna paradisaea)

The arctic tern appears darker gray than the common tern and has a blood red beak. Arctic terns migrate from nesting grounds in New England, Canada, and the far northern arctic regions all the way south to antarctica and back again each year. They are the champions of bird migration! Their nest is a scrape in the sand, or they may nest on small rocky islands of grass or gravel. Arctic terns usually lay two eggs which hatch after about 21 days. They feed on small fish, crabs, shrimp and sometimes insects.

Roseate Tern

(Sterna dougallii)

The roseate tern is one of the most beautiful birds in the world (at least I think so). It is gray above, but a silvery gray that looks almost white. Its breast and belly are pure white which turn to a rosy buff in spring. Its tail feathers are longer than other terns' and also pure white. The bill is black, although as the nesting season goes along, it gets a little orange at the base. Its legs are bright orange. The roseate tern is a federally endangered species. The largest nesting area in North America is in southern New England at Bird Island, off Cape Cod. Buzzards Bay is the largest nesting colony in the United States. Roseate terns usually lay two eggs which hatch in about 21 days.

When Summer was Over

The Common Terns and Least Terns that Billy came to know so well finished nesting on the beaches of Cape Cod in early August. For several weeks after leaving the nesting colony, the young birds flew over the sand dunes and open seas, following one or both of their parents. The adult birds continued to feed their chicks live fish, while the chicks began to practice on their own, diving into the water and trying to catch their own food. It was not an easy thing to learn to do.

By September and early October, the terns began to migrate south to warmer waters. They would spend the winter months along the northern coastline of South America, inhabiting beaches and river mouths from Guyana to Brazil. By winter, the chicks could feed themselves. Some would be far off shore diving for small fish, while others would stay near fishing boats along the shorelines and in muddy rivers, feeding off small fish that the fisherman would throw back into the water.

At the end of the winter, during March and April, the terns leave the tropical waters of South America and fly right back to the beach where Billy discovered them the year before. However, the young birds, now almost one year old, would stay behind. They would not be old enough to lay eggs and raise their own young until they were three years old.

People who live in the small villages along the coastline of South America sometimes eat terns. These people use nets to trap birds—not just terns, but all kinds of birds. All wild animals are constantly on the lookout for predators. Vern and Marsha told Billy about several predators that the terns watch out for in their nesting areas on Cape Cod. In South America during the winter months, people become the predators for these birds. Like all wild animals, the terns have to work very hard to survive.

These graceful "sea swallows" are fast, free and beautiful. If you visit the beaches of Cape Cod during the summer months, or the coastline and beaches of several states along our Atlantic and Pacific coasts, be sure to be on the lookout for these fascinating seabirds. Billy discovered them and got to know them, maybe you will too!

Reading List

Here is a list of books which have more information about terns: who they are, how they live, and how you can help to protect them. The first name is the author (the person or persons who wrote the book), next is the year it was published, then the title of the book, and finally the publisher. You can find these books at libraries, books stores, nature centers, or though the publisher.

Alden, P. and Peterson, R. T. 1982. **Peterson Field Guide Coloring Books: Birds.** Houghton Mifflin Co., Boston, MA.

Buckley, P. A. and Buckley, F. G. 1976. **Guidelines for the Protection and Management of Colonial Nesting Waterbirds.** National Park Service, Boston, MA.

Burnie, D. 1988. **Bird.** Eyewitness Books, Alfred A. Knopf, Inc., New York, NY.

Harrison, P. 1983. **Seabirds, An Identification Guide.** Houghton Mifflin Co., Boston, MA.

Hay, J. 1974. **Spirit of Survival.** E. P. Dutton & Co., Inc., New York, NY

Hay, J. 1991. **The Bird of Light.** W. W. Norton & Co., New York, NY

Kress, S. (As Told to Pete Salmansohn). 1997. **Project Puffin: How We Brought Puffins Back to Egg Rock.** Tilbury House, Gardiner, Maine. National Audubon Society, New York, NY.

Peterson, R. T. 1947. **A Field Guide to the Birds.** Houghton Mifflin Co., Boston, MA.

Richards, A. 1990. **Seabirds of the Northern Hemisphere.** Gallery Books, New York, NY.

Salmansohn, P. and Kress, S. 1997. **Giving Back to the Earth: An Activity Guide for Project Puffin and Seabird Colonies.** Tilbury House, Gardiner, Maine. National Audubon Society, New York, NY.

Schreiber, A. E. 1978. **Wonders of Terns.** Dodd, Mead and Company, New York, NY.

Terres, J. K. 1956. **The Audubon Society Encyclopedia of North American Birds.** Alfred A. Knopf, Inc., New York, NY.

Trull, P. 1992. **A Guide to the Common Birds of Cape Cod.** Shank Painter Publishing, Provincetown, MA.

Veit, R. R. and Petersen, W. R. 1993. **Birds of Massachusetts.** Massachusetts Audubon Society, Lincoln, MA.

Welty, S. F. 1971. **Birds with Bracelets: The Story of Bird Banding.** Prentice-Hall Inc., Englewood Cliffs, N.J.

Wharton, A. 1987. **Discovering Seabirds.** The Bookwright Press, New York, NY.

Zim, H. S. and Gabrielson, I. N. 1956. **Birds, A Golden Guide.** Golden Press, New York, NY.

Sources of Information about Protection for Colonial Nesting Seabirds

CALIFORNIA
Dept. of Fish & Game
1416 Ninth Street, Sacramento, CA 95814

CONNECTICUT
Dept. of Environmental Conservation
165 Capitol, Hartford, CT 06106

FLORIDA
Game & Fish Division
Route 7, Box 3055, Quincy, FL 32351

MAINE
Dept. of Inland Fisheries & Wildlife
P. O. Box 1298, Bangor, ME 04402-1298

MARYLAND
Dept. of Natural Resources
P. O. Box 68, Wye Mills, MD 21679

MASSACHUSETTS
Dept. of Fisheries & Wildlife
100 Cambridge St., Boston, MA 02202

NEW HAMPSHIRE
Fish & Game Dept.
2 Hazen Drive, Concord, NH 03301

NEW JERSEY
Division of Fish, Game & Wildlife
Box 383, RD-1, Hampton, NJ 09927

NEW YORK
Dept. of Environmental Conservation
Game Farm Road, Delmar, NY 12054-9767

NORTH CAROLINA
Wildlife Resources Commission
512 North Salisbury St., Raleigh 27604-1188

PUERTO RICO
Dept. of Natural Resources
P. O. Box 5887, San Juan, Puerto Rico 00906

RHODE ISLAND
Dept. of Environmental Management
83 Park Street, Providence, RI 02903

SOUTH CAROLINA
Wildlife Department
P. O. Box 167, Columbia, SC 29202

TEXAS
Parks and Wildlife
4200 Smith School Road, Austin, TX 78744

VIRGIN ISLANDS
Natural Resources Dept.
P. O. Box 4399, St. Thomas, USVI 00801

• You may also wish to contact your state and local Audubon Society.